# I'm a Bratty Ratty

## My Life as a Rat Terrier

### By Lucy LaPaglia

To order additional copies of this book, contact:
Xlibris Corporation
1-888-795-4274
www.Xlibris.com
Orders@Xlibris.com

Illustrator Kathleen Wilson has been "coloring" since her elementary school days!
With a bachelor of arts degree in visual communications and years of work
in graphic design, she is delighted to be able to spend her days
creating and, of course, coloring!
Kathleen lives in Austin, Texas, with her husband and their three children.


www.katykadiddlehopper.com

This book is dedicated to everyone out there
who has the privilege of owning a Bratty Ratty.
You are very blessed to own such a smart,
sneaky, loving protector like me.
Oh, and to my mom and dad who love me, feed me,
and take me for lots of rides in the car.
You are the best!

Love,
Lucy

My name is Brenda La Paglia, known to most as Lucy's mom.
I have a great job being Lucy's ghostwriter.
It doesn't pay in money but in lots of laughs and kisses.
She is the best companion a girl could have.
She sticks to me like glue, and she is by far
the best free thing (dog) I've ever gotten.

Enjoy,
Brenda

Dogs really do leave paw prints
on people's hearts.

I'm a Bratty Ratty.
Lucy is my name.
Life to me
Is one big game.

I live in an apple orchard
where I roam free.
I eat lots of apples
whenever I get hungry.

Two

Sometimes I stick my nose
places it doesn't belong.
That's when I remember
I should have listened to my mom.

She's always right, you know,
that's what I have learned.
If you play with fire
you're going to get burned.

Three

I got kicked by a mule
way up in the air.
That was one wild ride,
it gave me quite a scare.

I love to chase squirrels
or anything that moves.
Unless of course
it ends up having hooves.

I was chasing a cat
through the neighbor's yard.
My mom was chasing me,
she was running mighty hard.

She yelled at the top of her lungs,
"Leave that cat alone.
You're in big trouble, Lucy,
when I get you home."

Seven

It fell on deaf ears.
I had one thing on my mind:
To catch that darned cat
and make him mine.

My mom gets very angry
when I don't come.
She doesn't understand
that girls just want to have fun.

Ten

When the coast was clear
I snuck my way back home
because I'm not the kind of dog
who likes to be alone.

It was back to the doghouse
after I'd been caught.
As if you couldn't tell
I get in trouble a lot.

I ride on the fourwheeler
on the front seat.
One time I fell off
and rolled underneath.

I was covered in dirt
then I started to cry.
I never did that again
because I don't want to die.

Thirteen

I jumped back on
for the ride home.
For my bumps and bruises,
my mom gave me a bone.

It made me feel much better.
I then lay down for a nap.
I had quite a day
I was ready to relax.

Fifteen

My mom's one in a million,
she watches out for me.
That's part of her job,
keeping me safe and happy.

I'm a Bratty Ratty,
at least, that's what they say.
I'm just me, and I wouldn't have it
any other way.

Eighteen

# Lucy's Life Lessons

Apples are good for you.

Never play with fire.

Never stand behind a mule or a horse.

Don't make your mom so angry she has to chase you.

Come when you are called.

The doghouse or timeout is where lessons are learned.

Moms want what's best for you.

Twenty